THE FIGHT FOR
PLOVER HILL

EILÍS DILLON

Illustrated by Prudence Seward

THE O'BRIEN PRESS
DUBLIN

This edition published 2001 by The O'Brien Press Ltd,
20 Victoria Road, Dublin 6, Ireland.
Tel: +353 1 4923333; Fax: +353 1 4922777
E-mail books@obrien.ie
Website www.obrien.ie

First published 1957 by Hamish Hamilton Ltd.,
London, WC1

ISBN: 0-86278-709-2

British Library Cataloguing-in-Publication Data
A catalogue record for this title is available from
the British Library

1 2 3 4 5 6 7 8 9 10
01 02 03 04 05 06 07

The O'Brien Press receives
assistance from

The Arts Council
An Chomhairle Ealaíon

Layout and design: The O'Brien Press Ltd.
Illustrations: Prudence Seward
Colour separations: C&A Print Services Ltd.
Printing: Cox & Wyman Ltd.

The Fight for Plover Hill

EILÍS DILLON was born in Galway in 1920 and died in Dublin in 1994. Her award-winning books for children and adults are internationally renowned.

Other Eilís Dillon books from The O'Brien Press:

The Five Hundred
The Lost Island
The Cruise of the Santa Maria
Living in Imperial Rome
The House on the Shore
The Island of Ghosts

Also by the same author:

The Seekers
Down in the World
The Shadow of Vesuvius
A Herd of Deer
The Seals
The Sea Wall
The Singing Cave
The Island of Horses
A Family of Foxes

CONTENTS

CHAPTER ONE

EVEN after it had become an island, it was always called Plover Hill. Until then it had been a big, round-topped hill at the upper end of the long valley through which the Blackwater river flowed. Old Dan Flaherty's farm was on Plover Hill. His grandson, John, lived

7

in the village of Clooney, across the valley.

John's father was a carpenter. His house was the last one in the village. His workshop was built on to one end of it, so that all day long the house was filled with the sound of his saw singing and his hammer ringing as he made tables and chairs and window-frames and cartwheels for the whole village and the country around. He worked very hard, which was a good thing, because he had eleven children and they all liked to have plenty to eat. John was the youngest.

He and his grandfather were great friends. Very often, he walked down the path to the edge of the river, crossed the little wooden bridge and climbed up by the steep, stony road that led to the top of Plover Hill. It was never hard

to find old Dan. The farm was not big,
because a great part of the hill was covered
with trees and low bushes. In the grassy
places between, bluebells and buttercups
and primroses grew in spring, and clumps
of purple foxgloves in early summer.
This was the time that John liked best,
when the evenings glowed with warm
light and old Dan would stay out late
under the stars and tell him how he

had often seen leprechauns walking in solemn, busy procession close under the hedges, and how the foxes put on fox-gloves when they gathered for their summer dances. On these nights, John used to sleep in the farmhouse, in the bed that had been his mother's when she was a little girl.

Then the lake was made. One end of

the valley was closed with a dam, so that the river could not get out. It rose gradually higher and higher until it covered the long green meadows and crept up the hillsides and filled the whole valley from end to end. Then it spilled over the top of the dam in a huge, roaring, spouting waterfall.

"It's a fine thing for the country," said all the people. "Now we can have electricity."

And on Sunday afternoons they all walked out to stare at the dam and wonder at the wilderness of wires and towers that had grown up around it.

But John was not so pleased. Now Clooney village had its toes in the water. The path down into the valley, the little wooden bridge and the steep, stony road that led to the top of Plover Hill were all under the lake. There was a landing-stage with boats in front of John's house. Sometimes when his father took him out on the lake he could see deep down

through the water to where the path still showed clear and white.

Soon the people began to drop in for a visit to the carpenter's house, and to say to John's mother:

"How is your father, old Dan Flaherty, getting on, over on Plover Hill?"

"He's very well," she would say.

"When did you see him last?" they would ask.

"Not for a few weeks," she would answer. "It's not so easy to go to Plover

Hill now that it has become an island."

Then they said:

"You should bring him over to live in the village. It's not right for an old man to live all alone."

"But he's quite happy," she said. "He loves Plover Hill too much to leave it. He has never lived anywhere else, except when he was away on his travels."

"All the same," they said, shaking their heads and looking wise, "he should not live alone. It's a bad thing to be all alone."

Tom Connolly, who owned the big shop in the village, was very sure of this. He stopped John's mother as she was buying her groceries one Saturday, and said:

"I'll tell you what I'll do. I'll buy Plover Hill from your father. You go

over and tell him that. I can't sleep at night for worrying about him. You tell him that."

John looked up at Tom Connolly's mean, fat face and he thought he did not look in the least bit tired. He just looked mean and fat. One of his eyes was smaller than the other and this made him seem as if he were always planning something nasty. But John's mother did not think so. On the way home she said to John:

"Wasn't it kind of Mr. Connolly to offer to buy Plover Hill? With the money, my father could build a little house near us here in Clooney. Then we would see him every day. We'll go over tomorrow and tell him about it."

But when old Dan was told, he flew into a rage. He marched up and down and thumped the kitchen floor with his stick and said over and over again:

"I will not leave Plover Hill. I will not. I was born here. I'm going to die here. And that's that!"

As they rowed home in the boat, John could see that his mother was very distressed. She had begun to believe what all the people were saying, and still there seemed to be no way out.

Then John had an idea. He had it so suddenly that he jumped in the boat, sending it rocking from side to side and making ripples that washed away across the lake towards the shore.

"Easy on, man!" said his father, who was rowing. "I don't want to swim home."

"If I go to live on Plover Hill," said John, "he won't be alone."

His father laughed and said:

"You're too small."

But after a while he said:

"Of course, old Dan only wants someone to talk to. And he likes you. And we have ten more like you at home."

"Eleven is better than ten," said his mother quickly.

But after a while she agreed that John

could go, if his grandfather would have him.

"But you must come home if you don't like it," she said. "I won't let anyone sleep in your bed. I won't let anyone sit in your chair. If you get tired of Plover Hill you can come home, and we'll think of something else."

So it was arranged, and in the autumn John went to live on Plover Hill. Old Dan was very pleased to have John with him all the time.

"The leprechauns are not a very talkative crowd," he said, looking down sideways at John as they walked around the farm on the first day. "And I do get tired of talking to myself."

It was a wonderful life on Plover Hill. They had milk and butter from the cows. They had eggs from the fat red hens

that pecked all day around the big cobbled yard, and from the slim, brown ducks that paddled all day in the lake. Every Sunday morning, John's father rowed over from Clooney with tea and sugar and flour, and sacks of meal for the hens,

and sacks of cotton-cake for the cows, and everything else that was needed. Then he took John and his grandfather ashore to the church in the village, and at last, after a visit home, back to Plover Hill again. The old man was too old and John was too young for them to have a boat of their own.

Sometimes the cattle-dealer and the pig-buyer came in heavy motor-boats for the calves and young pigs. Everyone agreed that it was all very well arranged.

"And John will learn to be a farmer,"

they said to his mother. "That will be a fine thing, you'll see."

The only person who did not seem to like it was Tom Connolly. Every time that John's mother went into the shop, he came out from behind the counter to suggest more things that could go wrong on Plover Hill.

"It's not right to leave them there,"

he hissed in a low voice so that the other customers would not hear. "It's not right. It's not proper. You tell your father I'm still willing to buy the farm. You tell him that."

At last she got so tired of listening to him that she began to buy what she needed in the other shop, and she gave up going to Connolly's altogether.

CHAPTER TWO

IT was a fine life on Plover Hill, but boys must learn other things besides ploughing and harvesting and feeding calves and pigs. John had to learn to read and write and do sums. One day in the middle of winter, when the days were short and there was not much to be done on the farm, his grandfather took

him up to the little loft over the kitchen.
A huge tin trunk was standing there.
They lifted back the lid. Inside there
were all sorts of things that old Dan

had brought back from his travels when
he was a young man. He took out a
red leather belt decorated with great pieces
of chased silver.

"I had that in Mexico," he said. "I

had a whole set of red leather harness for my horse, too, with silver mountings. But it was too big to bring home."

Down underneath everything, there

were some faded school books. Old Dan took them out and piled them in a small heap on the floor. Then he picked one off the top and said with a sigh:

"I suppose we'd better begin with this one. I'm afraid I'm not much of a hand at book-learning."

"Never mind," said John. "I'll help you."

So they read Aesop's story of the donkey in the lion's skin, and John said:

"Our animals have more sense than to behave like that."

"But there are no lions on Plover Hill," said old Dan. "They might behave differently if there were."

Then he told John about all the things he had seen in Africa, where there are huge herds of zebra, which look very like donkeys, and the lions hunt them. He knew all about snakes, too, and leopards, and crocodiles. In no time at all they forgot about lessons.

In the spring, the people of Clooney

began to call on John's mother again saying:

"How is that small boy of yours getting on, over on Plover Hill?"

"He's getting on very well," she said.

"What are you going to do about school?" they asked.

"My father is teaching him."

"Old Dan? But he doesn't know enough to teach a boy. That boy will have to go to school. You'll have to do something about it."

When John came home for a visit on Sunday morning, his father and mother talked to him about it, and they talked to old Dan.

"I'm teaching him some things," said old Dan, "but I'm not sure if they are the right things. I think I know too much about animals and crops and poultry, and not enough about sums. When we do a sum about papering a room, or men building a house, somehow we always have the answer in cows and horses and sheep."

"That's bad," said John's father. "Something will have to be done about it, all right."

So on Monday morning he walked down the village to the school. The teacher was called Michael Kelly. He was very tall and very, very thin. He had only a little hair, and that grew to the back of his head where it stuck out like a crest. When he walked, he stooped a little forward at the shoulders and his head bobbed in and out so that he looked like a heron. But he had a kind heart and he was always in good humour, so it did not matter what he looked like.

He came out of the school when he saw John's father coming up the path. Inside, the boys went on singing out their lessons.

"There's my small boy John," said the carpenter. "He's living over on Plover Hill with old Dan Flaherty, so he can't go to school. He's going to grow up without learning how many yards it takes to paper a room, and how to write letters, and to name the principal towns."

"Can he read?" asked Mr. Kelly.

"Oh, he can read, all right."

"What else can he do?"

"He knows all about snakes, and crocodiles, and leopards, and about lions hunting zebra, and the kind of harness they use in Mexico."

"Those are all very good things," said

Mr. Kelly. "You'd be surprised. What else does he know?"

"He knows a lot about farming. Old Dan is well able to teach him that."

"I'll go over to see him," said Mr. Kelly, "if you'll lend me your boat after dinner."

So after dinner Mr. Kelly got into the boat and rowed over to Plover Hill. Old Dan and John saw him coming. They went down to the landing-stage to meet him and to help him to tie up his boat.

"He's not coming for nothing," said old Dan softly, as they watched the boat slide in by itself for the last few yards. "But there's no harm in him, so we'll hear what he has to say."

They took him up to the house and into the big stone-floored kitchen. They gave him the best rocking-chair to sit in.

"That chair belonged to my grandfather," said old Dan. "He was a big, long skinamalink like yourself, the image of a Johnny-the-Bog, not meaning any offence, so you should be comfortable in it. There's his picture beside you on the wall."

Mr. Kelly was not offended. Johnny-the-Bog is the country people's name for a heron, and he knew quite well that he looked like a heron. He swung around to look at the picture. It was an ancient photograph of a fierce old man with a spiky moustache and beard, in a big gold frame.

"He looks a fine man, what I can see of him," said Mr. Kelly with respect.

Old Dan was pleased at this.

"He was a fine man," he said. "He bought Plover Hill from Mr. Kennedy of Clooney House. When he died he left it to my father and my father left it to me. And when I die, John is going to get it, but I hope I'll live long enough to teach him how to farm it properly."

"Teaching," said Mr. Kelly. "That's what brought me over to visit you. That boy is not going to school. Everyone says something must be done about it."

"Everyone says, everyone says," said old Dan crossly. "If you ask me, everyone has too much to say. What they want is for me and John to leave Plover Hill and go over to live in Clooney."

"That might be the only way for John to go to school," said Mr. Kelly.

John pulled at old Dan's coat and said:

"Bring him out and show him."

"Would it do any good?" old Dan asked, looking down at him.

"I think it would," said John.

"Rise up on your two pins so, Mr. Kelly," said old Dan, "and we'll show you why we're not leaving Plover Hill."

Without a word, Mr. Kelly rose up as he was told to do. Old Dan led the way, stumping out into the lane and through the five-barred iron gate into the fields. John and Mr. Kelly followed him along the trodden path that led through more gates from field to field, until they came almost to the top of the hill. Here the fields stopped and the woods began. Wire netting fenced them off from the farm. Old Dan opened a little gate that led into the woods. The others followed him through, and he closed it carefully behind them.

The air was sweet with spring in there. They walked under the trees on a broad carpet of dark-green celandine leaves, starred with gold flowers. The bluebell leaves were growing in thick masses, and

the soft, wet moss on the tree-trunks had a wild, sharp tang. High overhead, the wind sang through the pine-trees' tops with a faint, roaring sound.

They had not gone three steps when

Mr. Kelly stopped and pointed excitedly: "There's a fox!"

There he was, sitting on his haunches, his ears cocked and his white chest gleaming against the green. Instead of darting away out of sight, he moved his tail slowly from side to side in a friendly way. Then he gave a short, high-pitched bark and began to run about in a small circle. They passed him quite close, but he just went on with his game.

The wood climbed upward for a piece, and then the ground sloped away again, down towards the lake. At the highest point there was a fallen tree-trunk. Old Dan sat on it, and invited Mr. Kelly to do the same. John sat between them.

"Now, quiet, please," said old Dan. "No shuffling the feet, no coughing or sneezing. Just quiet."

Mr. Kelly, being a school-teacher, knew what that meant. He sat perfectly still and looked calmly down towards the lake. The trees and bushes and wild grass grew all the way down to its edge. Now as he watched, little animals of different kinds began to come out of hiding and

to move through the clearings, cross-
ing and turning and scuttling about, looking busy and absorbed. John glanced

sideways at Mr. Kelly and was quite
satisfied with his astonished expression.

"These are all animals whose homes
were flooded out by the new lake," said

old Dan very softly. "That's a nasty thing to happen to a chap. I gave them hospitality here on Plover Hill. Dug a few

burrows myself, too, in the first days. Saved them a lot of time. This is all waste land, this part of the hill, so we let them have it for themselves."

"We have squirrels and rabbits and hares," said John, "and stoats and badgers and hedgehogs and otters. The otters used

to live under the banks of the Blackwater. They let me hold their babies. The grandmother otter once let me pet her."

43

"And the foxes?" asked Mr. Kelly softly, still with his eyes fixed on the swarming hillside.

"Foxes are very independent fellows," said old Dan. "It's no use expecting them to mix with the others. They like to feel free to make a raid and catch a rabbit now and then. That's why they stay apart." He paused for a moment and then said: "Now do you see why we don't want to leave Plover Hill?"

Mr. Kelly did not bother to answer that question. He thought hard for a while, never once taking his eyes off the moving pattern of animals below them. At last he said, on a long sigh:

"That's it, of course! Every holiday, I'll come over here and teach John myself. Then no one will be able to say that boy must go to school. School will come to him. That's what I'll do."

" 'Tis the answer, sure enough," said old Dan.

CHAPTER THREE

ONE evening, a few weeks later, John was walking in the woods when he saw a strange boat, tied to a tree-stump at the water's edge. He went down to look at it. He knew at once that it did not belong to one of the regular visitors to Plover Hill.

"An honest man would tie up at the landing-stage," said John to himself.

And he took the two short oars out of the boat, one at a time, and hid them in a bush. Then very cautiously he crept upwards through the thickest under-growth, watching to see where the boat's owner was.

At the top of the hill he lifted his head to look down towards the boat. He wanted to see if her owner had returned and was perhaps looking for his oars. It was all quite still down there, however, though a little wind was beginning to splash the lake water against the boat's sides. Then over on his left a bird flew up suddenly. There was the sharp, startling crack of a gunshot. The bird flapped away, squawking and showering tail feathers in a long stream behind her,

but he could see that she was not hurt. And out from among the trees came a man, carrying a gun. He carried it in an expectant way, as if he knew that there were plenty of other things to shoot.

John wished he were as tall as a pine tree and had eight heads, like the giant in a story he had just read. Then he would swing his mighty club and give that hunter something to think about. But since this was not possible he turned quickly and ran like a redshank back towards the house.

Old Dan was on his way out to meet him. They met in the field just beyond the wood and John said, panting and nearly swallowing his tongue in his hurry:

"A huge man, down there in the woods, with an enormous gun!"

"What's he doing?"

"He's doing murder," said John. "At least he will if we don't stop him."

Already old Dan was bounding through the gateway into the wood, so fast that

John had to save his breath to keep up with him.

They found the hunter, almost at the edge of the lake. He was crouched on one knee, aiming his gun intently at something that neither of them could see. With a roar of rage, old Dan charged down the hill. John galloped after him. Old Dan leaped on the hunter's back. The gun went off. Every bird in the wood squawked. John shouted. The hunter wailed and wriggled helplessly while John seized his gun and ran down to the edge of the lake with it, and threw it in with a huge, comfortable, satisfying splash. Then, suddenly everything was very still.

The hunter sat up. For the first time they saw his face. It was Tom Connolly.

He was all dressed up for hunting. He had a queer, round, corduroy cap with a short peak and flaps that he could pull down over his ears. He had corduroy trousers and gaiters, and huge, terrible boots with nails. He had a wide, loose,

waterproof jacket with big pockets for rabbits and little pockets for birds. All got up for killing as he was, his face looked extra mean and extra fat.

As soon as he could speak, he bellowed so that the birds in the trees fluttered again:

"My gun! My new gun! It cost forty pounds!"

"You may as well wave good-bye to your gun," said old Dan cheerfully, "for it would take a year to fish it out of the bed of the lake."

"I'll have the law on you!" said Connolly fiercely.

"Faith and I might have the law on you first," said old Dan, "for trespassing on private property."

Connolly stopped to think about this. Then he said:

"Anyway, it's a kindness to hunt on this hill, because it's alive with every kind of animal and bird you ever saw. I even saw plover."

"Of course," said old Dan impatiently. "Why do you think it's called Plover Hill?"

"Well you should thank me for getting rid of some of those pests for you. Over in Clooney I heard Mr. Kelly say that he never saw the like of Plover Hill for wild life. He said it was a wonder to the world. So I thought to myself that I'd come over to see it, and bring my gun for company. That's all I did."

"If you had left your gun at home, I wouldn't mind your coming," said old Dan. "I'll have no shooting on Plover Hill."

"But I saw foxes! They'll eat your chickens, your hens, your ducks, your geese, your turkeys. They'll even eat your young lambs."

"Nonsense," said old Dan calmly. "Fox knows better than to come around the farm."

"What does he eat, then?" asked Connolly in astonishment.

"Rabbits," said John.

"But don't you mind that? If you're so fond of rabbits, why don't you protect them?"

"Don't you try to make a fool of me," said old Dan sharply. "If fox catches rabbit, that's fox's business, and rabbit's business. That's the way of the world, and I'm not going to try changing it. I'm not going to disturb it. Fox doesn't use a gun. And talking about guns makes me mad again, so I think I'm going to throw you into the lake after your gun."

But John did not want this to happen. He could see that Tom Connolly was one of those people who believe that most animals were made for shooting at.

It was no use trying to change him. Throwing him into the lake would not make a better man of him. Besides, it might be dangerous to his health, though he looked so strong and hearty.

John said all this to his grandfather, while Connolly listened with great interest. At last the old man said regretfully:

"Well, I suppose we must let him go, then."

And Connolly was very glad to go down to the edge of the lake and climb into his boat and take his oars from John. Old Dan undid the rope that was tied around the tree-stump.

"Off you go!" he shouted.

And he gave the boat a mighty shove that sent it rocking out into the lake. He stood for a few minutes while he

watched Connolly frantically trying to steady the boat.

"I don't think we'll see him again for a long time," he said to John as they turned home.

CHAPTER FOUR

BUT old Dan was wrong. Three days later Connolly marched boldly into the kitchen while John and his grandfather were having dinner. This time, his grin was nearly as wide as the door, but his eyes were as hard as limestone pebbles after rain.

"God save all here!" said he heartily. He turned to call out through the open door. "Come in, come in, Mr. Kennedy, and sit down. Plenty of time, Dan, plenty of time to talk business when you've finished your dinner."

In through the doorway shambled Mr. Kennedy. John knew him well to look at, for he did all his shopping in Clooney. He was fat in a soft way, with woolly white hair and a gold watch-chain across his sagging waistcoat. He lived in the big house at the head of the valley. From a little distance away it looked a wonderful house, but when you came near you saw that the paint was patched with stains and the grass and weeds were growing right up to the front door. It had been a fine place once, at the time when old Dan's grandfather had bought Plover Hill from its owner. But the present Mr. Kennedy was lazy, and did not like to get his feet wet, old Dan always said, and he had let the house and farm go down.

They finished dinner to the sound of Connolly rocking up and down in the best rocking-chair. It seemed to John that his great-great-grandfather glared more fiercely than ever from his frame on the wall, as if he were not pleased to see his chair enjoyed by such an uncivil person. Then old Dan said:

"Go over to the far field, John, and see if the lambs are all safe."

John stood up at once and went out, because he could see that old Dan wanted to be alone with his visitors. He looked

at the lambs first and then he found several other things to do. Later he climbed a tree at the top of the hill, and sat on a high branch while the wind swayed him about to the sound of its own music. From there he could see the front of the house and the path that led down to the landing-stage, with the boat bobbing gently against it.

Presently he saw Tom Connolly and Mr. Kennedy come out of the house. Old Dan was behind them. John knew at once that his grandfather was angry, and he was sorry for this. He knew it was not good for him. It made him tired. The old man stumped all the way down the path to the landing-stage, thumping with his stick. But he pushed off the boat politely enough and this seemed strange to John. He climbed down and ran back to the house, so as to reach it just at the same time as old Dan.

They sat on the wooden seat outside the door.

"What did they want?" John asked.

"They wanted Plover Hill," said old Dan.

"But they can't have it," said John. "Plover Hill is ours."

Old Dan was silent for a while. Then

he said, seeming to pick his words very carefully:

"You remember I often told you that it was a shame for Mr. Kennedy to be so lazy about his fine house and farm."

John nodded. Old Dan went on:

"Well, you'll see when you're older that lazy people like to be comfortable and to have enough to eat, just like everyone else. They need money for this. But they don't want to work, so they have to find ways of getting things for nothing, and they often make other people work for them. So you can see that when Tom Connolly thought of this plan, Mr. Kennedy was very ready to agree to it. They say they are going to start a hotel in Mr. Kennedy's big house, and bring people over in boats every day, to shoot on Plover Hill."

"But they can't," said John again. "Or if they do, we'll have the law on them."

"The trouble is," said old Dan slowly, "that they say I don't own the whole of the hill, but only the part where the farm is. They say that when my grandfather bought the farm, he didn't buy the woods and the waste land at all. They say that no one cared about the wild part of the hill until now, so when my grandfather, and my father after him, behaved as if it all belonged to them, no one thought of stopping them."

"Then we must prove somehow that the whole hill belongs to us," said John.

"Quite right. You have a good head on you," said old Dan, and he began to look more cheerful. "It's a queer thing, but I was so put out when they were going away that I hadn't even the heart to swamp the boat on them."

"How can we prove that Plover Hill is ours?" John asked.

"I did hear once that there was a map," said old Dan. "It was a map of all the land that my grandfather bought, when he came back from America with his little fortune made. He was a fine, tough man, was my grandfather. Just look at him."

John turned to look into the kitchen at the picture. He certainly did look a fine, tough man who would not easily be deceived. Old Dan said:

"He would never have bought a farm without making sure that he knew where its boundaries were. We must find that map."

There and then they began to search. They went through every room in the

house, opening old cupboards and boxes and trunks until they had a huge pile of letters and papers on the kitchen table.

In the evening, old Dan lit the big, hanging oil lamp and settled down to read all the papers. Long after John had gone to bed, he still sat at the table. But in the morning he had to tell John that he had not found the map.

After breakfast they walked up the hill and into the woods. The sun shone through the new green chestnut leaves, speckling the soft, damp grass. In all the clearings, when they stopped to listen, they could hear the excited chittering of the squirrels overhead. Badgers bounded past, in that thundering way that they have. A hare stood tall on her long hunkers to gaze at them with her ears erect. A sly stoat flickered by. On the edge of the lake the otters had made a slide, and were tumbling down it one after another into the water. The old man and the boy sat and watched them for a long time.

"Shooting parties," said old Dan at last.

"You know, John, you heard me say many and many a time that I would never leave Plover Hill. But if shooting parties start coming here, we'll both have to go."

"That's true," said John. "We won't want to stay here, if that happens."

CHAPTER FIVE

DURING the next week, John thought of many plans for outwitting Connolly and Mr. Kennedy. He wanted to build a raft, so that he and old Dan could go up to Mr. Kennedy's house at the top of the lake, and creep on him while he was asleep, and tie him up, and roll him off somewhere out of the way. Or they could slip over to Clooney and steal all of Connolly's guns, and have them to defend the island with, when the shooting parties would start to come.

But old Dan would not agree to any of these plans. He said they were wrong,

and that two wrongs don't make a right.
At last John had to promise that he would
not do anything until they would hear
from Connolly and Mr. Kennedy again.

It was almost a week before they came
back. John was watching for them, as
he always was these days. He saw the
boat put out from the landing-stage at
Clooney and skim across the water,
straight and sure. As it came closer he

saw that as well as Connolly and Mr. Kennedy, there was a third man who was a stranger. He found old Dan at once and told him. Together they waited at the door of the house, while the three men marched up the path from the lake.

"They seem very pleased with themselves," said old Dan. "Let you run off and see how that last family of squirrels is getting on."

"I will," said John, "if you promise to be as tough a man as your grandfather."

"I'll try, anyway," said old Dan with a sigh.

John went off towards the hilltop, but he did not go very far. He knew that the baby squirrels were in the best of health and that they did not need him at all as much as his grandfather did now.

So when he had seen Connolly and Mr. Kennedy go into the house, he crept back very quietly and hung about as near as he dared to go. The kitchen window was wide open, because it was such a fine, warm day. Very soon he heard voices raised inside. He darted across to the house wall and stood under the window. Now he was glad to be small, for the top of his head only reached to the window-sill.

He listened for a while, but it was not easy to understand what was happening. Connolly was saying:

"You must sign that paper. Don't you hear the lawyer telling you that you must sign that paper."

Then the strange man's voice said:

"Really, Mr. Flaherty, I must advise you in your own interest to sign that paper."

Mr. Kennedy said:

"Go on, sign it, sign it!"

Then Connolly said, quite nastily:

"You keep out of it, Kennedy, or you'll ruin everything." Then, more sweetly to old Dan: "Well, take your time. Read the paper again. We're not in a hurry. We'll wait half an hour while you think it over. We'll walk around the island."

"No," said the lawyer. "We'll sit here while you read the paper again and think it over. Take your time, take your time."

"Take your time," bleated Mr. Kennedy.

John did not take his time. He flew

down the path to the landing-stage, hardly seeming to touch the ground with his feet. There was Connolly's boat, loosely tied up, with the oars lying along the seats. He saw with relief that they were

the same short oars that he had hidden in the bush only a few weeks ago.

He climbed into the boat. He fitted the oars carefully into the rowlocks before casting off, for he knew the danger of losing an oar. Then he leaned over and lifted the rope free, and began to push the boat off with his hands.

He had never used two oars together before, though his father had sometimes let him use one. He went at it very slowly and cautiously. The lake was as calm as a pan of cream, and there was no wind. Still the oars felt heavy and clumsy, and soon the palms of his hands were red and sore. But he never thought of stopping nor of giving up. It was slow, weary work. By the time he had tied up at the landing-stage in Clooney, he was afraid that most of the half-hour that old Dan had been given was used up.

On dry land, he wobbled at the knees for the first minute as he ran down the village to the school. He went so fast that no one had time to stop him and ask him why he was not over on Plover

Hill keeping old Dan Flaherty company, nor how a small boy of his size could have managed to row a boat even for such a short distance.

He had never been in the school before, but he had no time to be shy. He ran right in and pulled at Mr. Kelly's coat while he was in the middle of writing a word as long as a snake on the blackboard. Mr. Kelly bent down and John whispered in his big, red ear, while the boys in their desks watched in astonishment.

Mr. Kelly put down the chalk and said:

"Sorry, boys. I've got to go. Something very important. You'd better have the rest of the day free."

The boys were pleased with that, though they were too polite to let Mr.

Kelly see it. Before they had time to shout: "Good-bye, Mr. Kelly!" he was off up the street after John, to the landing-stage.

The journey back to Plover Hill only took ten minutes. The oars which had been so big for John looked tiny at the ends of Mr. Kelly's long arms. As they went, to help himself to sit still, John told him the whole story of the plan to take the wild part of Plover Hill from old Dan.

"And the wild part is the best part," he said. "They talk about it as if it were worth nothing."

"Tell me, why didn't you call your father instead of me?" Mr. Kelly asked after a while.

"When I heard that they had a lawyer, I knew we would need someone learned," said John. "That's what my grandfather always says, that it takes a learned man to outwit a lawyer."

"Your grandfather is a very wise man," said Mr. Kelly.

At the landing-stage, they hopped ashore, only pausing for a second to secure the boat. Then they galloped up the path to the house. This time Mr. Kelly was in front, looking more like an ostrich than a heron. John fluttered after him. The kitchen door still stood open. Mr. Kelly darted inside, and stopped. John, behind him, peered under his lifted arm at the scene.

Old Dan was sitting at the table, looking very tired. He was holding a pen in his hand. His bottle of ink stood open on the table before him, and beside it, all laid out, was the lawyer's paper.

Connolly was hanging over his shoulder, pointing out the place for him to sign. Mr. Kennedy and the lawyer were gazing eagerly at old Dan. All of them had their mouths expectantly open.

"Stop!" shouted Mr. Kelly.

Old Dan stopped. He laid the pen down on the table with a long sigh. Mr. Kennedy burst into tears and turned away. The lawyer shrugged his shoulders. Connolly ground his teeth and snarled with rage:

"Just when we had persuaded him at last!"

Suddenly he plunged forward from behind the table with his fist clenched to strike Mr. Kelly. His shoulder brushed against the picture of old Dan's grandfather and sent it crashing to the ground.

Old Dan leaped to his feet at the sound. They all turned to look at the picture.

It was in ruins. The glass was shattered. The old, worm-eaten frame had broken in a dozen pieces. Now, as they watched, slowly and deliberately the picture curled over at one corner and began to fall out of the frame. And there, pasted on its

back plainly to be seen, was a little faded map.

No one moved while old Dan stepped forward and lifted the picture, and laid it face downward on the table, on top of the lawyer's paper.

"There it is," he said. "A map of the farm, with the woods and the waste land, even a piece that's now gone down under the lake. I knew my grandfather was a fine, tough man. I knew he'd have put that map in a safe place."

"It was nearly too safe," said Mr. Kelly. He pointed to the door, and then to each of the unwelcome visitors in turn. John was almost a little sorry for Connolly as he gathered up Mr. Kennedy and the lawyer and took them away. Old Dan must have felt the same, for at

the last moment before they went off
down the path he called out:

"Connolly! I'll buy you a new gun.
But not for shooting on Plover Hill!"

He got only a growl of rage for thanks.

After that there was peace. Mr. Kelly
kept his word, and came over every day
of the holidays to teach John, so that
very soon he knew as much as any boy
of his age in the school. When he was
older and better able to handle a boat,
he rowed across to school in Clooney.
When he grew up and married, and began
to farm the land on Plover Hill himself,

93

there were always plenty of animals there, to sit at his fire among the children on winter evenings, and to dance and play for them under the summer moon.